PUFFIN BOOKS

Published by the Penguin Group: London, New York,
Australia, Canada, India, Ireland, New Zealand and South Africa
Penguin Books Ltd, Registered Offices:
80 Strand, London WC2R 0RL, England

puffinbooks.com

First published by William Heinemann Ltd 1986
Published by Viking 1999, reissued in Puffin Books 2002
036

Set in Adobe Bembo 23/26 pt

Made and printed in China

British Library Cataloguing in Publication Data
A CIP catalogue record for this book is available from the British Library

ISBN: 978–0–670–88624–1

Janet and Allan Ahlberg

THE JOLLY POSTMAN
or *Other People's Letters*

PUFFIN BOOKS

Once upon a bicycle,
   So they say,
A Jolly Postman came one day
   From over the hills
And far away . . .

With a letter for the Three Bears.

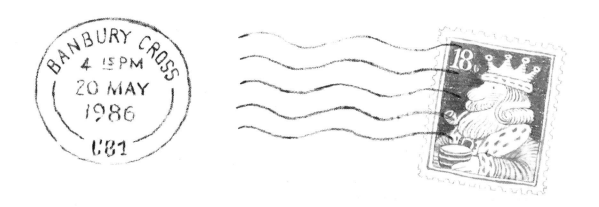

Mr and Mrs Bear

Three Bears   Cottage

The   Woods

So the Bears read the letter (except Baby Bear),
   The Postman drank his tea
And what happened next
   We'll very soon see.

Off went the Postman,
   Toodle-oo!
In his uniform of postal blue
   To a gingerbread cottage –
And garage too!

With a letter for the Wicked Witch.

So the Witch read the letter
With a cackle of glee
While the Postman read the paper
But *left* his tea. (It was green!)

Soon the Jolly Postman,
   We hear tell,
Stopped at a door with a giant bell
   And a giant
Bottle of milk as well,

With a *postcard* for . . . guess who?

So the Giant read the postcard
With Baby on his knee,
And the Postman wet his whistle
With a thimbleful of tea.

Once more on his bicycle
   The Postman rode
To a beautiful palace, so we've been told,
   Where nightingales sang
And a sign said 'SOLD',

With a letter for . . . Cinderella.
(There's a surprise!)

So Cinders read her little book,
    The Postman drank champagne
Then wobbled off
    On his round again
        (and again and again – Oops!)

Later on, the Postman,
   Feeling hot,
Came upon a 'grandma' in a shady spot;
   But 'Grandma' –
What big *teeth* you've got!

Besides, this is a letter for . . . Oooh!

So 'Grandma' read the letter
And poured the tea,
Which the not-so-Jolly Postman
Drank . . . nervously.

Now the Jolly Postman,
   Nearly done (so is the story),
Came to a house where a party had begun.
   On the step
Was a Bear with a bun.

But the letter was for . . . Goldilocks.

So Goldilocks put the pound note
  In the pocket of her frock,
And the Postman joined the party
  And they all played 'Postman's Knock'.

Once upon a bicycle,
   So they say,
A Jolly Postman came one day
   From over the hills
And far away . . .

And went home in the evening – for tea!

The End